With YOU

The Novella: Sculpt and Emily's Beginning

NASHODA ROSE

With You
Nashoda Rose

Published by Nashoda Rose

Toronto, Canada

Edited by Kristin Anders, The Romantic Editor
Formatting by Self Publishing Editing Service

Authors Note: This novella is the story of how Sculpt and Emily met. The novel "Torn from You" is what happens to them. "Torn from You" is a standalone.

Song Choice for "With You"
"In My Veins" by Andrew Belle (feat. Erin McCarly)

ISBN: 978-0-9917327-6-0

Chapter One

"Holy Christ Eme, look at that popsicle. Now that's Häagen-Dazs quality." Kat stood beside me, mouth agape, eyes plastered on Sculpt who was currently pounding into his opponent, The Obliterator. "Damn, he's totally fuckable. Like slam you against the wall fuckable."

She pinched my arm when I didn't respond.

"Oww." I rubbed the spot where her fingers squeezed my skin.

"You see those arms? I bet he could hold you up against the wall and fuck you without even huffing. Nix that, I want him huffing."

Sculpt was naked from the waist up, rippling muscles flexing with every punch. His long legs were agile and lean, able to move quickly compared to the other guy's slower bulk. Kind of like a Hummer against a bulldozer.

But, there was something about his eyes that had me watching him with breathless excitement mixed with a spritz of nervousness. They were dark, nearly black and piercing, as if he was looking right into his opponent and breaking him apart with his concentrated fearlessness. Shivers tap-danced across my heated skin, then a tweak of something hit my stomach. It felt like I was twirling in a field with my arms out and dandelion puffs were blowing all around me. A dizzying effect, yet beautiful and odd at the same time.

"You sure you want to do this?" Kat's voice tore me away from Sculpt who had just thrown The Obliterator onto his back and was pulling his arm back at an odd angle. "I'm all for hot guys, but he looks really scary. A hot scary, but still the hotness doesn't negate the scary cause he is oozing scariness. What about one of those classes? You know, the ones the college offers."

I'd already considered it, but waiting three months until classes started in September was not an option for me. I needed Sculpt's help now, and since Kat's brother knew him, it put him at the top of my list. Matt said the guy was in a rock band and was only fighting to try and make enough money to go on tour. Sculpt needing money was a bonus for me, because I was offering. Not much, but it was something.

"Matt says he's a good guy," I reminded her, but I was beginning to think he'd just meant the guy hadn't killed anyone yet. I think his answer would've been far different if he knew Kat and I were interested in actually meeting Sculpt.

My breath hitched as Sculpt pushed his damp hair off his forehead, his fingers weaving through the messy walnut strands. It was a casual gesture, but when he did it ... it was like my body was being infused with electricity. Why was I suddenly so hot? It wasn't like Toronto was scorching in June, although right now it felt over a hundred degrees and humid as hell.

"Yeah, Matt says that so he doesn't get the crap beat out of him." I laughed because Matt was over six foot, all muscle, and didn't take "crap" from anyone. "And if Matt finds out we're here, we're eating beets for the rest of the month." Kat's parents had passed away ten years ago in a drinking and driving accident. Unfortunately, it had been their dad who'd been driving drunk and ran into a cement bridge doing a hundred. Matt, being eighteen at the time, raised Kat on his own, and he cooked—Kat didn't. That meant he decided what to eat, and he'd totally give her beets for a month. And since I'd moved in with them two years ago, I'd get beets too, but I liked beets.

"Holy Jesus. You see that?" Kat started jumping up and down, screaming Sculpt's name with the rest of the young college crowd as The Obliterator lay unconscious on the ground. "One punch and down for the count. Woot. Woot. Woot," Kat shouted while pumping the air with her fist.

I clapped, but as I watched Sculpt, blood dripping down his forehead into his eye, and his chest glistening with sweat, my nerves crept up on me like a horde of white-tailed spiders. Kat was right, he *was* scary. The tattoo on his left arm extended from his shoulder down to his elbow. The dark black ink popped the images so they appeared three dimensional and vibrant. It suited him and made him totally ... fuckable.

I noticed Sculpt's eyes narrow and stare at something behind me. I glanced over my shoulder to see what held his attention so intently and expected to see some hot girl. Instead I saw an older man, maybe fifty or so, standing at the back of the warehouse looking right back at Sculpt. It was so obvious, everyone else was jostling one another or exchanging money, but not this guy. He stood like a statue—staring right back at Sculpt. His thin lips curved upward in slow motion. It wasn't a warm-and-fuzzy smile, more like a smile that made the hairs on the back of your neck stand at attention, begging to be plucked so they could run for their lives.

Sculpt's body stiffened. Maybe others wouldn't have noticed, but I did, because when he ran his hand through his hair this time, it was completely different. His fingers were curled and his nails looked like they would've dug grooves into his scalp. When he lowered his arm it was unsteady and slow—rigid.

I glanced back over my shoulder at the guy. The man had this evil glint in his tapered eyes, and his thin lips were pressed together so hard that his bottom lip nearly disappeared. He was wearing a suit; odd considering they were in a filthy abandoned warehouse with mostly college kids.

Lip-guy gave one nod to Sculpt then turned and started to leave. He was surrounded by five men who looked like they were part of the underground fighting ring. I tugged on Kat's shirt. "Who's that? The guy leaving."

Kat glanced over her shoulder toward the door and shrugged. "No idea, but ..." She froze, eyes widening. "Fuck. Fuck. Fuck. Matt."

"Shit." When Matt got mad, it wasn't just a few short curse words, it was a lecture that had us both hanging our heads and shifting our feet.

Matt's face grew fierce when he noticed us. We were too far away to tell, but I knew two red blotches were burning bright on his chiseled cheekbones. It was the kind of face that would make Godzilla tuck his tail between his legs and run.

"On the burner," I muttered.

"On high," Kat replied.

Matt began shoving people out of his way as he strode toward us. It looked like he was pushing car-dashboard spring dolls, people popping right back in place after he passed. And not a single one of them gave him attitude for it.

Kat squeezed my forearm. "Go. I'll intercept him while you ask scary hot-ass." She licked her lips, and her eyes shimmered like aventurescence. "If he helps you ... you so have to fuck him."

I rolled my eyes, typical Kat. "Owe you, missy."

"Sure do. I fucking hate beets."

I smiled then ducked and weaved my way through the crowd. I heard Matt shout my name and picked up the pace until I'd made my way around to the other side of the warehouse where I'd last seen Sculpt.

I stopped, stood on my tip toes and peered past the crowd. Sculpt stood ten feet away with an arm hooked around a girl's waist. Blonde, tall, and wearing what looked like a spandex miniskirt that barely covered her ass. If you could even call it an ass; more like a pancake.

Okay, Sculpt didn't look so scary now. The hard lines of his face had eased—somewhat. I was never very confident when it came to guys. Bullies, and an alcoholic mother who called me ugly and told me I ruined her life put a big dent in the self-image.

You get made fun of enough times about your weight, you start to believe it. Wide Load was my nickname in grade seven. Grade eight, Gavin Hochman changed it to Balloon Butt, which wasn't so bad really ... okay it was bad, but I got used to it. My height had finally caught up to my ass in grade ten, but I wasn't a toothpick. I still had an ass, but I also had hips and curves which Kat said was every guy's wet dream. I still wasn't so sure about that, especially when all the magazine covers had models looking like the girl currently hanging off Sculpt like a piece of tinsel.

Seriously, the guy was too attractive for his own good. The tinsel on his left arm glared at me as if I was going to steal her Christmas tree. I wanted to stick my tongue out at her, because, really, I was no competition for her. Sculpt obviously liked rail-thin, legs-to-the-ceiling, make-up-heavy chicks, and I was ... well, not.

But my purpose was also far different than hers.

I pressed closer and touched the tip of my finger to his arm. He completely ignored me. The girl snickered and slapping her was feeling like a real good idea. I may be unconfident around guys, but I was the complete opposite with girls my own age.

I tapped again—harder.

"Sugar, one sec." Sculpt didn't even turn his head and continued talking to the two guys in front of him.

I glanced over my shoulder and saw Kat chatting to Matt who was wildly searching the crowd for me. Shit, I needed to do this now.

I looked at the girl. "Umm sorry, but I haven't seen my brother in a really long time. Would you mind giving us a minute?" I smiled sweetly. "Please." I raised my brows for that doleful effect, and I could tell she bought it as she slipped from his grasp. The funny thing was, he didn't even notice, or if he had, he didn't care.

The girl backed away, although she stayed close enough to make certain her claws could still reach him.

My turn. I wrapped my fingers around his bicep, well, *wrapping* was an exaggeration as they couldn't even come close to circling anything on him except maybe his baby finger.

I tugged while squeezing. "Sculpt?"

He spun around looking on either side of him for the missing girl, then his eyes ran the length of me as if I was up for auction. He looped his arm around my waist and tugged me in tight. I heard the tinsel girl huff then her high heels clicked on the cement floor as she stormed away.

Sculpt leaned in so his lips were close to nibbling on my ear. My breath hitched, and a vibration went through my body. I wasn't sure if it was from nerves or something else entirely, then I decided it was both. "Not my type," he said in a deep throaty whisper. "Too young, and I don't do ..."

Short. Boring. Drab. The words never left my mouth, instead I did what I always did when guys used to make fun of me—I curled my toes.

"Brunettes," he finished.

Oh. I pulled back, and he let me, but his arm remained around my waist, hand resting on my hip. Dry mouth was rearing its ugly head as I stared up at him, taking in the slight curve of his nose, his angled cheekbones ,and God, he had this dimple in his chin I wanted to run my finger across.

"Where'd the blonde go?"

To find more bleach for her hair.

"You scare her away?"

His breath tickled the sensitive place just below my ear, and my nerves shot off so violently that I knew I'd have fallen flat on my face if he'd let me go.

"Um well no, not exactly. I told her I was your sister and needed to talk to you."

His brows rose and he wasn't smiling ... Shit. "Sister? I don't have a sister, at least not one I'm aware of. Unless you're trying to tell me something?" There was an edge to his voice; rough with a hint of darkness.

My mouth gaped. "No. God, no. I'm not your sister. It's just ... I wanted to talk to you alone."

His gaze dripped down my body then back up again. I felt like a piece of steak, and he was appraising me to see if I was worth the price. "So, if not my sister then what do you want from me?"

The reason fled my mind, and I stood staring at him like that stupid piece of steak. "I ... ah ... well." His tongue slid across his upper lip wetting the surface and making it glisten. Jesus, did he even know he was doing that?

"I'm not going to fuck you. I may fight illegally, but I don't fuck illegally."

My sudden mind boggle vanished, and ire replaced it. "I'm twenty for your information, and I wouldn't even consider having sex—"

He frowned, and his lips pursed together. The look sent a flush into my cheeks, because honestly, the guy looked even hotter with a scowl. "Having sex? Can you even say the word fuck?"

"Yeah. Fuck you."

Silence. Then he laughed; his dark eyes sparkling like black opals. The sound was utterly magical, and several people nearby looked at Sculpt with surprise.

God, this was a waste of time, and now Kat and I would be peeing red for the next month. I turned to leave, but his hand snagged mine.

"Why'd you come looking for me?" His tone was gentler with a pinch of graveled sexiness which didn't help any.

Okay, I couldn't let Kat eat beets without even asking him; she'd make me eat hers, and I didn't like them *that* much. "I need to learn how to fight."

"Excuse me?"

"I want to fight."

"You're kidding, right?"

I shook my head.

He laughed again, his head thrown back and the sound echoing in the warehouse. I could feel the heat rising in my cheeks, and despite the fact that he was laughing at me, I was more mortified that I was turned on by his laugh. "You're scared as shit of me. Shoulders slumped, confidence of a mouse ... You're not going to make a fighter of any kind."

"I don't want to fight like you or anything. I just need to know a few moves."

"Then go take a class. I don't have the time to teach some chick how to pull a punch." He let my hand go and chin-nodded to a guy who walked up to shake his hand.

"Nice take down, buddy."

"Thanks. You see those men?" Sculpt was now completely ignoring me; I'd become invisible.

"Sure did."

"You get who they were?"

His friend nodded. "I'm guessing. Fuck man, not cool. How'd do you think he found you?"

"Hey," I said. He ignored me, and I grabbed his arm. "Hey."

When he turned my stomach went through the roof of my mouth. His eyes honed in on me, and I nearly slunk away under his penetrating glare. "Classes don't start until September, and I need them now."

"No." He looked down at my small hand holding him. "Let go."

I shook my head. "I need this."

His eyes narrowed and mouth tightened. "Is your boyfriend hitting you?"

"I don't have a boyfriend."

"Then why the hell does a girl like you want to learn how to fight?"

I looked down at my feet, shuffled a bit then met his gaze dead on. I had no choice. "I was attacked after work by a guy and—"

"He rape you?" His tone was scary deep, and his eyes darkened with that intense gleam that wouldn't let me look away even if I wanted to.

"No." But the guy managed to pull down my jeans, tear off my thong and put his finger inside me. I'd bit his hand covering my mouth, and when he pulled away, hand raised to slap me, I'd screamed so loudly that he took off.

I never reported it, even though Kat begged me to, and we kept it from Matt because he was mega overprotective. Maybe that's what happens when you take on the role of father at an early age. Kat and I say he's a popcorn kernel waiting to pop. When we suspect he's going to blow, we say he's "on the burner."

So, telling Matt was a bad idea. Besides it'd been dark, and he took me down so fast, I had no idea what he looked like. All I knew was he was big, bulky big, with breath smelling like cigars and mints.

Sculpt was quiet for several moments then he said, "They catch him?"

I shrugged looking down at my feet again. "No." I took a deep breath. Maybe this *was* the wrong guy to ask. All I could think about was his rough hands touching me, his lips hard against mine, the little nibbles on my ear, and his breath tickling my heated skin.

Suddenly, Sculpt grabbed my hand and curled my fingers into a fist. "You think you can hit someone. A guy wanting to get a piece of you? With this? You weigh a hundred pounds max."

A hundred and twenty actually.

"Fighting won't help you, Mouse. Haven't you heard of the buddy system? Staying clear of dark places at night? My answer stays the same—no."

I bet if that tinsel girl asked for his help, he'd have leapt at the chance. I tried to not let it bother me; after all I was used to being the girl who had no friends until Matt and Kat. Their parents' deaths coinciding with my father's within months of one another had formed a bond between us that was unbreakable.

So why would a guy like Sculpt help me? What had I been thinking asking him?

"She's Kat's friend." The guy who'd been talking to Sculpt interrupted. "You know ... Matt's little sister." Sculpt's attention drew away from me for a mere second, and I breathed a sigh of relief. It was exhausting keeping my emotions under control with him staring. "Saw her with Kat earlier," Sculpt's friend continued. He held out his hand, and I took it. "Hey, I'm Kite."

"Hi. Emily." I half-smiled.

Kite nodded to the right. "Well Emily, you piss off Matt? Cause he looks none too happy, and he's headed this way."

Sculpt looked in the direction Kite indicated. "Jesus."

"I'd say," Kite muttered. "Looks like a mouth flogging for you, Emily."

When Sculpt turned back to me, my stomach bottomed out. Everything in him was tense, even his jawline was pulsating. "Are you dating him?"

"He's my best friend's brother and my roommate. No, of course not."

"He's pissed man. And now he's looking at you." Kite chuckled. "I'm betting he thinks you're hitting on her."

Sculpt grunted. "Not a chance."

I blanched, feeling like an ant he'd just stomped on. No matter if I already knew that he'd never *be* with me, hearing it aloud felt like I'd breathed in acid fumes and was decomposing. What an ass he was for throwing it in my face.

"We need to leave." Sculpt snagged my hand. "Tell Matt I'll take her home."

"Um, what?" I tried to pull from his grasp, but it was like a being held by a tree.

Once again he ignored me as he tugged, and I stumbled after him. The crowd parted for him like the red sea as we made our way to the door.

He didn't slow until we stopped beside a black racing bike. The black metal reflected in the moonlight while the chrome surfaces were so polished they looked like mirrors. He undid a steel cable on the back, grabbed a helmet, then plopped it down on my head. He proceeded to do up the chinstrap before I could even begin to process that he was riding off on his bike and taking me with him.

He threw his leg over the seat and started the engine, the loud purr sending vibrations through my body. I'd never been on a motorcycle and hadn't intended on ever riding a death trap on wheels. I stepped back, my fingers undoing the strap.

He caught my wrist. "Get on, Mouse."

"Yeah, um, I'm going to pass." I'd rather bungee jump than get on a motorcycle. At least jumpers had a cord attached to their legs, a bike had nothing—no seatbelt, no essential airbags.

"You want me to teach you how to fight, but you're scared of getting on a fuckin' bike? Jesus." He glanced toward the warehouse door then back at me. He tugged me close with one pull. "Get your ass on the bike, and I'll give you one lesson. One. Then we will see, but I hear a single cry, whimper, whine, or complaint, then I walk."

Harsh and rude—but fair enough. No chance was I saying no. "Okay."

"Okay." His brows rose as I stood staring at him astride the racing bike. "Move it, Mouse."

The tingling between my legs worsened, and the butterflies in my stomach were having an all-out party. The thought of getting on behind him, feeling Sculpt up against me ... Well it had my body reacting in strange, scary ways.

"Now."

"Ah, yeah." I approached the bike then skimmed my leg over the back, instantly feeling the tremors run through me. No wonder guys liked bikes; they were a total turn on.

He half-turned, reached back, placed his hand on the small of my back and roughly shoved me forward until my pelvis was up against his ass and the inside of my thighs were against his outer thighs. Heat shot through me.

"Arms." He grabbed both wrists and tucked them around his waist. "Tight, Mouse."

I squeezed, feeling his hard abdomen beneath my hands.

The bike shifted to the side, he reeved the engine, and we took off.

Chapter Two

Five weeks later

"Mouse, you're not listening to me. Jesus. Get your hip behind me." He had me flat on my back for the seventh time today, his hands holding my wrists above my head.

It was our fifth lesson, and every week I'd complained, bitched, and cried—after Sculpt dropped me off at home, and I was alone.

"Screw off. I'm trying my best." My confidence was building; Sculpt made sure of that by peeling through my fears like an onion.

At least now when he pretended to choke me, I didn't squeal and freeze up in panic, instead I raised my arm overtop of his and jammed my fingers into his trachea.

He was tough on me, and more often than not I was spitting mad, which I was slowly realizing he liked. If I was mad then I wasn't scared, and that, to him, was far better, because at least I'd fight back then.

"Well try harder. I'm not wasting my time if you're going to dick around."

"Dick around? Really? Did you just say that?" He also could push my buttons. I tried to shove him off me, but with his hands holding my wrists, and sitting on top of my pelvis all I managed to do was look like a trapped writhing eel. "Do you think I like landing on my back continually?"

Sculpt raised his brows, a hint of a smile playing at the corners of his mouth. It was the first time I'd seen him smile. Since the night he laughed at me, I'd never seen anything other than him being serious. He was kind of a quiet guy with his words and his emotions. It was like he was hiding behind his scowl. But seeing that twitch of a smile had me so turned on I swear I felt dampness between my legs.

A lock of his walnut hair fell in front of his left eye, and I wanted to push it back then run my fingers through the thick strands. I called it sexy bedroom hair, because it always looked like hands had been running through it. Maybe they had. God, how many women had their hands in his hair? A strange tightness gripped my chest at the thought. Jealousy? Shit, I had no right to feel jealous of anyone. Sculpt would never be interested in me. What was I thinking?

"Emily?"

I just knew if he kissed me with those perfect lips that it would be the single best experience of my life. Okay, I was only twenty, but still I'd been kissed by guys, and I couldn't imagine them being better kissers than Sculpt. Not that he'd even consider kissing me. "The Sculpt" as the women screamed when he entered the ring, could get any woman he wanted. And from the blonde I'd witnessed, they'd be nothing like me. They were prime rib, and I was pork chops.

"Lego building."

I jerked at his words. "What?"

"You think too much."

"So? I have a lot on my mind. And what does Lego have to do with it?"

His dark eyes narrowed. "You build up blocks in your head in techno color."

He was right—I did. I knew I was way out of Sculpt's league, but I couldn't help imagining him doing more than knocking me onto my ass time and again. Since we'd spent two to three hours a week together I thought I'd get over this little infatuation, but I didn't. It was getting worse, and it was getting worse because we were going for ice-cream after practice, eating our cones while sitting on the curb beside his bike, and he was texting me every day. I really had no clue why he texted me; it was just a quick check in, and it pissed me off, because now whenever my phone vibrated my heart went on a hundred-mile run.

"Did I hurt you?"

I shook my head and met his gaze. He was staring down at me with hooded eyes; they were dark because he was still a little pissed, and his brows lowered over them. And he had these great eye lashes, black and a little long for a guy, but it totally suited him. No wonder I couldn't concentrate. He was the ultimate distraction.

"You need to pay attention." He gripped my chin with his thumb and forefinger. "And you should be out shopping, not in this filthy abandoned barn with me."

I'd chosen a place just on the outskirts of Toronto. I often came here when I managed to snag Matt's car. I'd sit up on the hill just north of the barn and watch the horses. I'd been coming here for two years, and the herd had grown to thirty-two horses; most of them looked like quarter horses—palominos, pintos, and my favorite the appaloosa—like wild mustangs.

Besides, I'd take a filthy barn with Sculpt any day over shopping. When Kat managed to bring me to the mall with her it was like being dragged slowly across gravel on a sweltering day—naked. Pure torture. She had to try on everything then hum and haw over whether it fit right or if the price was right or if she actually needed it. More often than not, Kat put it back on the rack after spending fifteen minutes trying to come to a decision.

I was feeling pretty confident with the self-defence moves Sculpt had taught me, even though he'd laid me flat on my back a few thousand times without even blinking. It hurt. I had bruises to prove it. But if some guy attacked me again, I at least had some clue as to how to defend myself instead of trembling like a washer on spin cycle.

His thumb stroked back and forth across my chin. I swear he had no idea he was doing that delicious, small movement. But my body new it, felt it, and it was pissing me off. I hated that he could do that to me. I felt out of control, and he was no doubt completely unaware of how he was making my insides burn, my heart race and my skin tingle with shots of electricity.

The last time we were eating ice-cream after our practice, a drip of vanilla escaped the corner of my mouth. Sculpt gently wiped it away with the pad of his thumb before I had the chance to use my napkin. He went back to crunching on his sugar cone while I tried to get control of my body's reaction to his intimate touch. My only saving grace was that Sculpt never seemed to notice my response to him.

"Eme?" His tone was sharp and agitated.

"I'm paying attention, okay?" I snapped. His brows rose with surprise, and my heart stopped dead then dove into a racing force of beats. "But you sitting on top of me, your hands holding me down, and you looking at me like that ..." His eyes smoldered, and his lips parted. "Damn it, I'm not fucking immune, okay?"

"Emily."

I knew he had no interest in me; I was younger by four years, and he could get any girl he wanted. There was no sexiness about me. God, I didn't even own a pair of high heels. Plus I was a brunette.

His head lowered as he leaned forward. Eyes watching me. Hands on my wrists sliding over my palms until our fingers interlocked.

"Eme."

I turned my head to the side, not wanting him to see my glistening eyes. "It's fine. Just get off me." And then I lied—big time. "It's not like I'm interested or anything, cause I'm not—at all. You have a shitty track record, you're cocky, and I hate guys that fight."

"You know nothing about me." His tone was harsh, and I quivered beneath him.

"Well, you're hot. And I'm sure you know it, which is so unattractive." I'd purposely avoided going to see Sculpt's band play at Matt's bar, because Sculpt singing on stage would be my kryptonite.

I certainly didn't need another reason to drool over him; it was already embarrassing. "I bet you have girls hanging off your every word. Probably after a fight you walk down a row of girls and pick the one you want for the night. How many have you slept with? A hundred? No, you're a lead singer in a band, so I'm betting more." Was I blabbering? Damn, I was. Where was my dry mouth when I needed it? God, I sounded absolutely ridiculous. "Listen, I don't care what turns you on. I need to get home."

His fingers tightened around mine. "You."

"Me what?"

He lowered further, and I could feel his breath on my face, the sweet scent of him dragging into my lungs with each inhale. "I don't sleep around, and you turn me on."

"Me?" My voice cracked, and my chest heaved in and out.

"Yes."

"What?" Was my skin tingling? It felt like I was on fire. Were we on fire? Was the barn burning down?

"You heard me."

"Oh." Holy bejesus. Five weeks he'd been teaching me self defense, and in those five sexually frustrating weeks I'd been dreaming of him kissing me, touching me, his hands gripping my thighs as he pressed me against the wall, his mouth devouring every inch of my naked body.

He leaned in further. I swear my breath was sucked from my lungs by some mysterious, high-powered vacuum that was hanging above me, because I couldn't breathe. Being scared and excited does something to your body. The emotions put you into overdrive with trembling limbs, heart pounding, and that sweet ache between your legs. I knew how to satisfy myself, but this ... this could put my orgasms to shame, because this guy rocketed my body into another dimension.

"Shh, relax Mouse." The scruff on his face rubbed against the underside of my chin as he kissed my neck. "I've been taking you down on the mat for five weeks now ... feeling your curves beneath me." He kissed my ear, a nibble on my lobe that sent a spark right through my body, and my fingers tightened around his. "I don't play games, Eme. If you feel what I do then your time is up."

"Um, what does that mean?"

"It means I don't screw around. No games. You're into me, so now I'm taking you."

Holy crap. I was trembling, and all I could think about was him taking me. "Okay."

"I wasn't giving you a choice. Too late for that."

"Oh."

He kissed my chin, then along my jaw line. "Eme, you're something sweet, and I want sweet. Wanted it for a while now."

Damn it, kiss me, I screamed. Bad, wrong, or whatever, I wanted him to kiss me.

He pushed back, and I panicked, eyes widening at the thought he was going to leave. Instead, Sculpt stared down at me for several seconds, then released one of my hands and stroked the side of my face until his finger reached my jaw line.

"I kiss you Emily ... there's no going back. No other guy kisses you, touches you, or gets to taste what's mine. I don't share."

I started to laugh but quickly frowned. He didn't look like he was joking. "You're serious?"

"Yeah, Eme, I am. I don't share, and I don't like to lose—ever." My mouth gaped with shock. Was he kidding me? No, he looked serious, and he was distracting me again with his finger tracing over my ear and then down my neck and back.

"I'm not something to win, Sculpt."

He huffed. "Yeah you are, Mouse. You're a trophy. I've known that for weeks."

I gasped. Wow. Just wow.

His finger drew a line down my neck into the hollow then over my collar bone and kept going. "This part right here." He circled his finger right above the crevice between my breasts. "Is hot. When you're turned on, Eme, it heats up like your cheeks." He leaned down and kissed the spot, then his tongue traced where his finger had been.

"Sculpt." My breathing was harsh, and I felt as if my insides had just been set off by a land mine. "Sculpt."

He raised his head, and his eyes were magnificent, blazing with lust. "Yes?"

He didn't wait for a response as he trailed kisses up my throat until he hovered over my mouth, barely touching, both of us breathing hard. I lifted my head to try and reach his lips, but he moved back, and I moaned with frustration.

"What's your full name, Emily?"

"Emily McAughtrie."

"Emily McAughtrie" The way he said my name sent shivers sprinting across my skin in a heated fever. "I'm going to kiss you now, Miss McAughtrie."

His mouth came down on mine before I had time to suck in air, and it was hard, possessive and ... all encompassing. His tongue slipped between my lips then swirled within the heated wetness. He let go of my other wrist, and my hands came down to touch him— fingers curling in his hair while the others caressed his back, feeling the muscles flexing beneath his T-shirt.

His hands were everywhere, holding my head as he deepened the kiss, then running down the side of my body. Every part of me was alive in that one moment. He was ruining me for all other men. There was no other guy who could ever make my body feel more alive than Sculpt did.

"Eme." He kissed the corner of my lips, then my eyes, then my temple. "This needs to stop."

"No." I pulled him down, tilting my head so his lips could take mine again. He groaned as ours mouths met, and I sighed beneath his warmth, suckling on his tongue and sinking my fingernails into his back and dragging down.

It was like I was starving. I couldn't get enough of him. Comparable to living in gray for years and suddenly Sculpt had woke me up, and I saw a rainbow of color.

He suddenly rolled over and threw his arm over his face, his breathing erratic, chest heaving. "No, Eme. We need to go."

"Oh." Did he not like my kiss? I knew I wasn't that experienced, but it felt like he'd been into it.

He must have heard the disappointment in my voice, because he was up on his side, taking my hand and looking down at me. And those eyes ... His expression was soft, and yes, there was a hint of frustration, and his brows were drawn together.

"Mouse, I'm not fucking you on the floor of a barn, and if I don't stop kissing you, I *will* fuck you." I bit my lip to stop myself from smiling—he liked the kiss. Sculpt jumped to his feet and held out his hand. "I'm taking you home. And tomorrow, you're hearing me play."

"I am?" His voice already turned me on. I couldn't imagine him singing, what it would do to me.

He hauled me to my feet and swept my hair back over my shoulder, his fingers lingering on my neck. "I'll pick you up after work tomorrow." His fingers laced with mine, and he walked me out of the barn.

I stopped dead. The horses were grazing on the hillside. The sun was setting over the horizon, and their coats glistened in the orange rays. Magnificent.

Sculpt moved behind me, wrapped his arms around my middle, and pulled me snug against him. "I see you looking for them the moment we drive up. They're something special to you, aren't they?" His words whispered across my ear, and I shivered. God, hearing him sing ... I was going to lose myself to him.

"Yeah. I love them." And then I told him my dream, one I knew was just that—a dream. I was practical, and I knew horses were a luxury. I'd have to win a lottery to have my dream come true. "I want to have my own horse farm one day. I'd take in abused and unmanageable horses and teach them how to feel beautiful and proud again."

He moved in closer, and his finger tucked my hair back behind my ear. "A trophy, Eme."

The lead mare lifted her head and whined, her flank quivering with her call. The brilliant sleek chestnut started trotting up the hill, and the others followed.

I came here whenever I could, learning how they communicated, watching their body language with one another. I'd even been taking riding lessons for the past two years, and the owner of the barn let me work off payment by grooming the horses. I'd spend the rest of my life on a horse farm if I could, but instead I was going to college for accounting in September. My dad used to say, "Princess, you've a head for numbers. My little accountant." So, I was hoping to get my accounting license then maybe get into a corporate company. Matt said when I graduated I could be his accountant for the bar, but I wanted to do this on my own. I'd relied on Matt enough throughout my life in order to get away from my mother.

Sculpt licked the tip of my ear lobe, and a thrill of excitement swept through my body. "I'll bring you here anytime you want, Emily."

Was I crazy believing that this guy liked me? Why did he want me when he could have any girl? I wasn't even a blonde for God's sake.

I followed him to the bike, then slid on behind him. His hand squeezed my thigh, and I stopped fiddling with my helmet strap to look at him.

"It goes both ways, Mouse."

"What?"

"If I have you, I'll never touch another woman."

Chapter Three

The next day I was making my last espresso before ending my shift when I heard the ding from the door and Georgie's gasp of, "Get me some new panties." She always said that when a hot guy came in. "*Well* ... look who it is."

Georgie owned the coffee shop. She was twenty-four, with pink streaks in her hair and probably more tattoos than Sculpt. She was also sweet, sassy, and her no-bullshit attitude had many men dropping their jaws. I think she tried to shock them and took delight in making them squirm. The only one she couldn't make squirm was Deck, a friend of hers. I don't even think Deck smiled.

But Georgie had no trouble trying her skills on the newcomer. "Hey there delicious. Been a while. What can I put between your sweet lips?"

I sputtered a laugh, turning with a steaming hot cup in my hand. The second my eyes hit Sculpt my breath seized. He stood at the counter in overly worn blue jeans and a white T-shirt with his sexy bedroom hair messy from the light breeze. He caught me staring, and his eyes darkened which sent a twinge deep in my womb. He winked then met Georgie's engrossed gaze. I almost fainted at seeing him wink; it just wasn't Sculpt. He was stoic and stern, not playful.

"Just Emily, Georgie."

Georgie's eyes widened, and then she looked over her shoulder at me. "Don't tell me the make-out worthy eye candy you've been gabbing about for weeks is Sculpt?"

"Oh my God," I muttered beneath my breath, utterly humiliated. My hands shook while I poured a shot of milk into the cup then walked over to the side counter and slid the espresso to the waiting customer. Georgie obviously knew who Sculpt was, and by Sculpt's words he knew her. Wasn't really surprising; Georgie knew a lot of people.

My cheeks felt like they'd been set on fire, and when I glanced over at Sculpt he was staring at me expectantly. "Make-out worthy? Did she say that, Georgie?"

Georgie's brows rose revealing her dark gold-and-purple eye shadow. "Oh yeah. Girl's been panting over you for weeks." Then she leaned forward, both palms flat on the marble surface of the counter. "But being a cupcake doesn't mean you know how to treat a girl. And I know you Sculpt, you don't know how to treat a girl. Shit, don't even remember you being with a girl. Treat this one like fucking crystal. She's something special. You hurt her, you're hurting me, and you know where hurting me leads."

I walked up beside her. "Georgie," I pleaded, hearing every word.

"Emily," she retorted, standing up straight.

Sculpt looked completely undeterred by Georgie's warning and met her steady gaze dead on. "I know she's something special. Just have to convince *her* of that." My personal rabble of butterflies took flight. "Not many women shock me. Eme did. Even better is underneath the mouse, I suspect lives a lion."

"Ha. Yep. Don't I know it." Georgie put her arm around my shoulders and squeezed. "Break her heart ... Well, Deck isn't going to be happy. I think you know what he's capable of."

"Georgie, please." I rolled my eyes and shook my head at Sculpt. "She's kidding." Although, I knew she wasn't. Deck was scary.

Sculpt appeared to take her threat seriously though and nodded. "Where is he? I've been trying to reach him for weeks. Need him to look into something for me."

She shrugged. "Gone. You know how it is."

"If he contacts you, tell him to get in touch with me."

Georgie's eyes narrowed. "Yeah? Not liking the sound of that."

"Need a call, Georgie." His voice had gotten scary deep, and even Georgie paid attention to it, giving him a nod.

I'd known Georgie only a few months, since I'd started working at Perk Avenue to make some money before college. I also knew Deck checked up on her all the time.

She hated it, said it made her feel like a kid. I'd noticed he always scanned the shop and even went to check in the back as if he was searching for explosives or something. Georgie merely shrugged when I asked why he did that every time he came by.

Deck didn't take her shit and continued to do it no matter how much she bitched—and Georgie knew how to bitch. Deck came by routinely, took his coffee black, and had yet to say anything besides Georgie's name. Cold, stoic expression with a tribal tattoo running down the side of his neck, Deck looked fierce. The short buzz cut with a good amount of scruff on his face finished off the look. But his eyes were what softened his face as they drooped in the outer corners and were the brightest green I'd ever seen.

Except in the last few weeks Deck had been "out of town." I wasn't sure what that meant, but his absence was something significant, because Georgie accentuated the "out of town." Deck being gone didn't mean Georgie wasn't checked up on; it meant another guy came by, and he was just as frightening as Deck.

Georgie always appeared unperturbed by Deck's appearance and rarely looked at him as she handed him his usual coffee. He left five bucks on the counter for it every single time, even though Georgie tried to refuse it. She never put it in the cash register, instead slipped it into a kid's pink elephant bank she kept under the counter.

"Mouse, let's go."

"Um, yeah." I looked at Georgie, and she waved her hand.

"Go with your make-out-worthy guy. I'll see you tomorrow." She gave me a hug and whispered in my ear, "Careful, sweetie. He's something different. Don't want to have to send Deck after him ... Deck can be a real dick. Sculpt's face being fucked up—be a bitchin' shame."

I knew Sculpt was different, and that was why I wanted to take it slow. He was closed off and never talked about his family or his past. I figured maybe it took him a while to open up. Well, it wasn't like I shared either. I had told him that I no longer saw my mother, but I hadn't offered any explanation and thankfully he hadn't pushed. At the time, I'd thought that had been odd. Most people would immediately ask why, but Sculpt never said a word. Maybe because he didn't want to have to reciprocate and talk about his family.

I grabbed my purse, and Sculpt took my hand as I came around the end of the counter. His pinkie finger swept aside a stray strand of hair from my forehead, and from the way his eyes took me in, I swear my panties got damp.

"Where're we going?" I asked as he led me outside.

He stopped beside a rusted old truck. "You're going to hear me play." He opened the door, and it creaked on its corroded hinges.

I jumped up onto the old vinyl blue seat and reached out, my hand touching his chest before he moved away. "Are you any good? Cause I hate whiny voices and am not a fan of the screaming hard rock stuff. Gives me a headache, actually."

He leaned in close, his eyes flashing, and the corners of his mouth curving upward. God, I wished he smiled more often. "When I scream Eme, you'll love it. And I won't be giving you a headache, I'll be taking it away."

Holy shit. A deep ache moved into my womb and settled in like it was staying for a while. Damn it, I was putty in his hands. *Please don't hurt me. Please don't hurt me.* I'd lost the only family I had in the world —my mom didn't count, and I didn't want to go through anything even close to being so cutting again as losing my dad.

My dad had been my rock; my mom the hammer smashing the rock. Dad called me his little princess; mom called me the garbage that ruined her life. Of course she never said that when my dad was around. It got worse after my dad died of lung cancer when I was ten. Then she became a full-time bitch, and that was when I started running away to Matt and Kat's who were dealing with their own grief at the time. Sometimes, my mom didn't notice I was gone for a good twelve hours. She missed me when she needed something done, and suddenly I wasn't around to do it.

Sculpt's mouth was so close I sucked in his breath as I inhaled, and it made my body come alive. I couldn't imagine what was going to happen when I heard him sing. All thoughts vanished as his hands came on either side of my face and held me still—not that I was going to go anywhere with him standing there looking at me like I was the only woman in the world.

"Give me your mouth, Eme."

Even if I could have found words, he stole them away as his lips lowered over mine. His kiss was slow and hard, yet sweet and lingering. Our mouths moved together in harmony, and the throbbing ache between my legs intensified.

I wanted him.

Needed him.

He groaned as he pulled back, and my body went with him until I caught myself and sat back in my seat, breathing hard, feeling as if my thirst hadn't been satisfied. And it scared the crap out of me. I had a feeling being thirsty would be the worst sort of torture anyone could experience.

"I ... Sculpt you're ..." What was the word? "Overwhelming and—"

"Quiet, Eme." He quickly kissed me on the lips before I could protest. "Buckle up." He shut the door, and I leaned back in the seat and sighed.

As I watched him walk around the front of the truck I realized there were so many reasons why I was attracted to him. There was no bullshit with him. He was real, and even though sometimes it threw me off balance, it was refreshing. What I respected most was how he was determined and focused. He'd told me his dream was to make it with his band, Torn. He did the fighting in order to make that happen, and even though he hated it, he did it with everything he had in order to make his dream happen. There was no half-ass with Sculpt.

What I found adorable was his addiction to vanilla ice cream, and when he ate it ... It was like his entire body completely submitted to it.

His playful smile, when he rarely let me see it, left my knees quaking, and when he looked at me ... when he really looked at me ... his eyes lit up like fireflies. It made me feel special, and I hadn't had that since my dad passed.

Sculpt drove us to the park, and I sat leaning against a large oak tree while he lounged beside me with his guitar in his lap. He hadn't even strummed or sang a note, and I was feeling like my insides were melting under a firestorm of heat.

His head tilted to the right as he picked at the strings one by one. I was mesmerized, and each second I waited for him to sing was perpetual agony. This guy had me kidnapped and strung up in him without even trying, and it terrified me.

He looked at me, his hands quiet on his guitar. He was frowning, and for some reason it was hot. Super-hot. I wanted to kiss him so badly that it actually hurt and that right there is why it terrified me.

He looked at me. "You have that look. Like you did when you asked me to teach you how to fight ... scared as a fuckin' mouse. What's up?"

His scent trickled into me as his hand reached up and stroked the side of my face.

I looked down at my fingers playing with the hem of my shirt. "What's happening between us ... I don't know what it is. It ... scares me." Sculpt has such big plans. Would I get in his way? I wouldn't be a burden to anyone anymore. I wanted to make it on my own, and in a way Sculpt had given me more confidence to pursue my independence by teaching me how to fight.

He frowned, and I tried to lean back, but his hand cupped the back of my neck stopping me. "Sculpt, I don't even know your real name. It's just that—"

"Stop."

I shut my mouth, because I rambled when I got nervous, and Sculpt was catching onto that.

"My past isn't important. There's nothing to talk about. I want you. That's it, Eme. That's what's important."

Only my dad had ever wanted me and having Sculpt tell me he wanted me ... made my insides light up. I really didn't know how to respond, so I didn't, and neither did he. It wasn't awkward; it never was between us. Silence with him was a gift, and I think we both got that.

When Sculpt began to play, his voice completely knocked me flat on my ass, captivated me from the second he started singing. It was deep. It was graveled and raw. And it was sexy as hell. His eyes closed while the music pulled him in, soft bedroom hair drifting across his forehead as he lost himself in the words.

God, it was stunning. It was beautiful. And he held me hostage with his voice. It was like the wind was carrying me on his words, and I floated in a realm of captive magnificence.

If he could do this to me, I could only imagine what happened when he got on stage with his band.

He stopped, and my mind was still replaying the sound over and over again. I was lost within his voice, the beautiful way his fingers skimmed over the guitar strings with ease. It was so natural and raw.

His hand lay flat against the guitar, and his eyes were on me. I licked my lips then moved in close until I was a breath away from his mouth. We were both breathing heavy as we stared at one another. I felt like I was sucking him into my lungs, tasting him on my tongue.

"You're the reason music exists," I whispered. I pressed my lips against his and heard him groan against them. It vibrated into me, and the butterflies in my stomach did a drunken dance.

I couldn't get close enough with the guitar between us, but at that moment it didn't matter as long as Sculpt kissed me. His mouth swept me up into him like his voice had, bringing me to a place of no return. I was lost to him even if I thought I could stop it. I knew this was it. If he hurt me, I'd be shattered crystal. He could do that to me, and yet, I didn't care. It was worth the risk. He was worth the risk.

"Mouse," he moaned pulling back. "You wet, Eme? Is your pussy throbbing?"

I felt the heat in my cheeks inflame, and I lowered my gaze from his. He knew exactly what was happening to me, and yet it was still embarrassing to hear it aloud.

"God, you look sexy as hell shy and sweet. Now answer the question."

I nodded.

He groaned then kissed me again, but this time it was quick and soft. "You ever had sex before baby?"

I shook my head and lowered my eyes from his. Why did that feel embarrassing? Probably because he'd had sex numerous times with girls who knew what they were doing.

"I like that, Mouse. I like that a lot. Means you'll only ever be mine."

Sculpt ended up playing me three more songs as I sat astride his legs and watched. He wasn't nervous at me staring at him so closely; instead he seemed to thrive on it. I wondered if this was what he felt on stage. Did he love the fans, the screaming girls, all the attention? I really had no idea how popular he was, but Matt's bar was well known in Toronto, and I suspected Torn did well enough.

When the sun started to sink behind the city buildings, Sculpt put his guitar away.

"So, you know Deck?" I wanted to know more about Sculpt, and since he never talked about his family then I figured I may get a glimpse of his past through his friends.

His hands stilled on the latch of the case then proceeded to lock it. "Yes."

"And Georgie?"

"Yeah."

I was getting the impression that expanding on the subject was going to be like pulling a horse from quicksand. "Why are you trying to get a hold of Deck?" Georgie said Deck had a company involved with tracking down not-so-savory men. I wasn't sure what he did with them after he caught them, and Georgie was pretty close-lipped about it.

"It's not something I'm talking about, Emily."

"But Deck is—"

"No." He cupped my chin, eyes delving into me. "I'm not talking about it."

He looked really serious, and I knew Sculpt enough by now that if I pushed when his eyes were dark like that he'd shut down, and I hated when he did that. I felt locked out.

"When are you leaving? To go on tour?"

I knew he was saving money from fighting to pay for the band to go on tour, but I was uncertain how long before he'd have to leave. We really hadn't discussed it past him telling me he'd be eventually leaving. But "eventually" could mean anything and I wanted a timeline. I needed to be prepared for the hurt that'd come with it.

"Soon."

Oh God, I wasn't ready to lose him when I just found him. "Soon when?"

"Not sure. Depends on how many fights I get."

"But you have an idea?"

He nodded. "Couple months, maybe sooner."

"Oh." He put his hands on my hips and tugged me in closer. I tried to act nonchalant as I said, "Well, that's good then."

"Mouse."

"No, really. That's great. You should be out there. Your voice is ... It's truly stunning, Sculpt. You'll be a huge hit one day."

"Mouse." His hands tightened.

I barely noticed his frown as my mind whirled with uncertainty. What was I doing? Sculpt was a fighter. A soon-to-be rock star. I was just plain Emily with a dream I couldn't reach. I shouldn't even be thinking about more than today with Sculpt, but I couldn't help it. I was thinking what would happen in two months. Would he just leave and that would be the end?

"Emily."

I jolted, and his hands were now cradling my head, and he was staring intently at me. "You need to get it in your head that you're something special. I don't know how you got this bullshit about being a nobody in your head in first place, but I'm tempted to hire a plane with a banner saying how special you are."

"Sculpt! That's ridiculous."

"You thinking you're not special is ridiculous, Eme." Sculpt ran his thumb over my lower lip then leaned in and kissed the same spot. “I’m a fighter, Mouse. And I know what I want in life, and I’m not scared to take it. I want you. I’m not walking away from you. When I go on tour and you’re here, then you’re still mine and no one touches you. Okay?”

I nodded, because really when his voice got all low and scary, I wasn’t going to argue. Besides, I only wanted to be his.

“These lips are mine.” He leaned in and kissed me—hard. So hard it stole my breath and made my body tremble.

“Will you promise me something?” I asked when I caught my breath.

“You don’t need promises from me, Mouse. My word is always good.”

“If you’re leaving, don’t just leave ... I mean will you come tell me? To, you know, say goodbye?”

“Eme.” He roughly took my chin in his hand and made me look at him. “You’re getting the plane with the trailing banner.”

I huffed.

“If a guy ever treated you like that, I’d kill him. Then I’d give you a piece of my mind for going out with a piece of shit.” His fingers tightened on my chin. “I’m not letting you go. Okay?”

I nodded.

“Good.”

When Sculpt dropped me off at home, I hadn’t expected Matt and Kat to be waiting up for me. And I knew as soon as I walked into the living room and saw Matt’s tense jaw, pursed mouth, and messed hair that he was upset.

Kat sat on the couch, her short blonde hair swaying forward to cover her brilliant sea-blue eyes as she watched me. She was a classic beauty; smooth and flawless skin, thin brows, and sharp features. But her classic look was opposite of her personality. Kat was spontaneous, reckless, and she'd had numerous men in the last two years, none of whom stayed longer than a few weeks.

Kat mouthed, "On the burner."

Shit.

"You're working late. Again." Shit. I hadn't told him about Sculpt yet. Matt's arms were crossed, and his legs were braced. "You going to explain to me why Sculpt is talking to me about you?"

I awkwardly sat on the edge of the couch, and glanced at Kat beside me who quirked a smile and rolled her eyes at her overprotective brother. "Well ... we've been kind of—"

"Tell me you're not fucking him, Eme."

"Jesus, Matt," Kat said and reached over and squeezed my hand. "It isn't any of your business who Emily's with."

"Like hell it's not. Sculpt's bad news, and I don't want you anywhere near him."

Kat slapped her hand onto the leather couch making a loud smacking sound. "Bah. Matt don't be absurd. You said so yourself a few weeks ago that Sculpt is a good guy."

"Yeah, for showing up on time for his gigs, paying for his fuckin' drinks, and bringing me business with his band. Christ, the guy even keeps his bandmates in line, but I sure as hell wasn't saying he's a good guy for my sister's best friend." Matt ran his hand through his hair, took a ragged breath, and walked over and crouched down in front of me. "Emily." He sighed. "I know after your dad ..." He took my hands, and his thumbs rubbed back and forth on the back of them. "I know what it's like to lose a parent, and sometimes when you miss them you end up looking for a replacement of sorts. Someone to ease that missing link. Sculpt isn't that guy. Has he told you anything about his past?"

I shook my head.

"That's because not a single person knows anything about it. He is closed off, and that means he's dangerous."

"He's friends with Georgie, and he knows Deck and—"

"And he's been playing at my bar for months, and no one knows his real name. Not even his bandmates. I don't like it, Emily."

Ever since grade school when Kat and I had started hanging out, Matt had been there for the both of us. I'd snuck in Kat's bedroom window numerous times after running away from my mom's when she brought a new boyfriend home. Matt never kicked me out, never told me to go home, nor did he call my mom. Instead, he bought me a cell phone, programmed his number in it, and told me if I ever needed to leave home that I was to call him, and he'd come get me.

I loved him and Kat; they were my family, but I saw in Sculpt something Matt couldn't. I saw the truth in his words. The meaning in his touch and the sweetness in his kiss. There was something more to him than he let everyone see. A vulnerability beneath his confidence.

"Matt," Emily said. "I get why you're worried but—"

"Oh I'm more than worried, Emily." He stood and walked toward the kitchen where he opened the fridge, grabbed a beer, and popped the cap. "You're not dating him."

I stood, hands on my hips. "Matt."

"No, Emily. You live under my roof, you're following my rules."

Kat gasped jumping to her feet beside me. "Matt. No."

Anger pulsated, and I strode over to him but stopped just out of reach, afraid of getting too close and slapping him. "I pay rent. You have no say over who I date. And I'm dating Sculpt."

Matt slammed his beer down on the counter, and it foamed up over the sides. His face was beet red as he glared at me. But I wouldn't on this. "No, you're not. Jesus, Emily, he's a fuckin' illegal fighter. I already dragged Kat out of that underground shit and you ... you took off on his fuckin' motorcycle." Oh. I guess he saw us leave. He hadn't mentioned it, and I certainly wasn't going to ask. "Yeah, I saw you. I spoke to Kite who told me you didn't want to be there and just needed a ride home. Sculpt provided." *Thank you, Kite.* "I let it go, because he brought you straight home, and you weren't hurt."

"God, Matt we're not kids anymore." Kat came up beside him and placed her hand on his arm.

His gaze turned to her, and his brows rose. "You wanna go there, Kat? Beets not enough?" She scrunched up her nose and made a face as soon as he turned back to me. "End it, Emily. Now." He picked up his beer and strode from the kitchen. I could hear his feet pounding up the stairs to his room.

I jumped when the door slammed.

Kat put her arms around me, and I slunk into her embrace. "Don't worry. He's just shocked, that's all. Give him time. He's never seen you date before, and Sculpt is ... well Matt is just worried. Give him a few days, he'll settle."

I didn't think so, and I was guessing Kat was just trying to make me feel better. Since I'd moved in with them on my eighteenth birthday two years ago, this had been the first fight Matt and I had, and I really didn't like pissing him off. Matt was very protective. That's why Kat and I had never told him about my attack a couple months ago. Well, Kat had wanted to, but I insisted otherwise. I knew how responsible he felt toward both of us, and it would have only hurt him to know that he hadn't protected me. Even though he wasn't to blame—at all. Matt was the type of guy who took all the responsibility onto his shoulders. Guess that happens when you're so young and need to suddenly grow up and become a parent to your ten-year-old sister.

Kat went to the fridge, pulled out two beers, and cracked off the caps. "So, you going to tell me what's up with you and Mr. Fuckable?" Kat passed one to me, and we tipped the necks, clanking them together. "'Cause last I heard, he was slamming you onto your back in some old barn."

I took a swig of my beer and smiled. Then I told her.

Chapter Four

I fell harder each day we spent together. Harder than I wanted or maybe should have, but Sculpt was protective and sweet in his own way. And cocky and demanding. He liked to call it self-assured and challenging.

I'd discovered Sculpt's passion stretched beyond vanilla ice cream to motorcycles. There wasn't once when we passed an ice cream parlor that we didn't stop for a scoop, and when he saw a parked motorcycle he liked the look of, we stopped and he admired. It was cute. I liked it—a lot.

He picked me up every morning to take me to the coffee shop. I disputed that the TTC and I were old friends, and it wasn't a big deal taking public transit if it was too late at night to walk. He said no. Of course I said, "Don't be silly," and he raised his brows and gave me that *don't argue with me* look. I glared. Then he kissed me and had been picking me up ever since.

I was concerned about Matt seeing Sculpt pulling up on his bike at our place. Most of the time Matt was at his bar when Sculpt dropped me off at night, but in the mornings he was home, and

Sculpt's bike wasn't the quietest of vehicles. I never mentioned the argument Matt and I had to Sculpt, hoping that Matt would settle in to the idea.

He hadn't yet.

We went for dinner at the Brazen Head in King Liberty Village. It was a nice restaurant, and I knew Sculpt was saving his money, but he wanted to celebrate the new song he'd written as it was inspired by me.

I tried to persuade him to take me to his place and I could make him dinner, but he told me his place was off limits. That unsettled me a bit, considering I had yet to meet his band, see where he lived, and he still never talked about his past.

Of course, I knew about his band, and he talked about them. Internet became my best friend when I'd met Sculpt, and I'd tried to find out everything I could about him, which included Torn. I scrolled through pictures and blurbs about them. Ream was the lead guitarist, Crisis guitar, and Kite drums. I also read that Crisis was an ass, "offensive" according to one blurb in a local paper. When I mentioned it to Sculpt, he grunted and said Crisis had the article hanging in his bedroom.

Sculpt ate the Jambalaya and had ice cream for dessert. I squirmed in my chair while he licked the remnants of vanilla off his lips, giving me that "look" when he finished—intense eyes, soft mouth, sitting back in his chair, relaxed and casual, arm slung over the back. I felt like I was naked, and he was slowly running his tongue inch by inch across my skin.

I was so turned on by the time the bill came that I stumbled as I shoved back my seat and knocked it over backward. Sculpt chuckled while reaching for my chair, which set me on fire more becausc I rarely heard him laugh, and it was throaty and deep and sent my pulse racing. He slipped his arm around my waist, leaned in and whispered in my ear how much he wanted to slip his finger between my legs and feel how wet I was ... My breath hitched, and I swear my body combusted, and I had a mini orgasm right then.

Then he whispered, “Soon, I’m sinking into that wetness, Eme. But not yet.”

“When?”

The corners of his lips twitched. He knew exactly what he was doing to me. “When I know your first time will make you scream my name, Mouse. When I know I have you completely.”

Didn’t he know? He already had me completely. I just wasn’t ready to tell him that. Maybe that was what he was waiting for?

By the time we walked outside, my chest was heaving and my blood was racing through my veins like heated honey. We made it two strides toward his bike before he snagged my hand, shoved me hard against the brick wall and devoured me.

A rush of urgency ripped through me. It was instant relief and release as his mouth drove into mine. His hands grabbed my wrists and pressed them against the wall above my head. Trapped by his heated hardness on one side and the rough, jagged brick on the other, I submitted to him completely. It was pleasure and pain on every part of my skin, and I couldn’t get enough.

He groaned, and the vibration had me quivering beneath his kiss as it sunk straight into my bones.

Nothing was said when he broke away, but when our eyes locked I saw the possession, his need, and I knew I looked the same. We were somewhere neither of us had been before, and it was an utter loss of control.

Back at my place, I wished we stayed longer at the restaurant ... Well outside the restaurant. I took off my helmet—Sculpt had bought one just for me—and hooked it onto the back seat with the steel cable. When I looked up at him still sitting on his bike, his head was tilted and a lock of hair had fallen in front of his eye. My stomach’s permanent butterflies airlifted and hovered. I sighed, leaning into him, hands pressed into his thigh.

“Are you going to tell me your real name? I mean Sculpt can’t be what your parents named you.” I wanted to know who Sculpt really was, and he was cagey about his childhood, his past. The only thing I knew was that Sculpt's best friend was Kite, and he considered the band his family.

"I don't use my real name, Eme. Haven't since I was sixteen."

"Why? Is it something that doesn't suit a fighter rock star, like Elmer or Herbert?" I giggled trying to imagine fans screaming the name Elmer at one of his fights.

He shrugged. "No one except Kite knows it. And it's staying that way." His tone was sharp, and I knew I'd touched a sore spot.

I deflated. It was disappointing that he kept a part of himself closed off from me. It hurt, and my confidence took a blow because of it. Maybe Matt was right.

The hardness in Sculpt's face slipped away, and his arm slipped around my waist. "Do you need that plane flying by your window?"

I smiled.

"My past is real shit, Eme, and I'm not polluting you with it." His phone went off, and his arm dropped away from me as he pulled it from his leather jacket pocket then scrolled through the text message. "Fight tonight, Mouse." He typed something, then slid his phone back into his pocket, and linked his hand around the back of my neck, drawing me in for a kiss.

All thoughts of finding out his name vanished as his mouth roamed over mine in a slow, luxurious awakening. It was much different from the wild, out-of-control kiss earlier, but it was so hot and sweet, and I melted into him. He could have me anyway he wanted.

I sighed in disappointment when he pulled away.

"I want to go with you." I didn't particularly like the fighting, but it was better to hate watching him fight than to stay home wondering and not knowing if he was okay.

"No." He started his bike, reeving the engine.

I placed my hands on my hips and raised my brows. "No?"

"Yeah, Eme. No. I don't want you around those people."

"So, I don't have a say in this?"

"No." He sighed, lowered his head, and looked back up at me. "Eme, I don't want you hurt."

"Hurt? You're the one doing the fighting. And I want to be there. I want to make sure you're okay. It'll kill me to stay at home wondering if you're injured. Please, Sculpt."

He shut off his bike and stared at me for a few seconds, his face expressionless. Then he grabbed my hand and lifted my left leg over the seat of the bike so I was facing him. His hand drove into my hair and yanked back.

I gasped at the pain that instantly became pleasure. Then his mouth came down on mine. It was possessive and raw, almost painful, but it stole my breath, held it captive, and chained me to him.

He groaned, hand tightening in my hair as he nipped at my lower lip, kissing me again. My thighs were over the top of his, my pelvis was digging into his groin that was hard and pressing into me. Damp panties were riding into my crotch, and my limbs were shaking as only Sculpt could do to me with a single kiss. There was no going back. This was it. This was him, and even if he never told me anything about his childhood, I belonged to him.

"What the fuck?" Matt's voice shouted as the front door slammed so hard the house probably shook. He strode toward us, and I quickly hopped off the bike.

"Sculpt, go." He ignored me and climbed off then put his hand on the small of my back "What are you doing? He's going to kill you."

Sculpt's brows rose. "Eme, really?"

Okay, that was stupid, but Matt was a big guy, and I really didn't want to see two men I adored fight one another. I went to stand in front of Sculpt to intercept, but he caught my hand and pulled me behind him.

"Sculpt," I objected.

"Mouse."

"Emily, get in the house." Matt stopped abruptly in front of Sculpt, his shoes making a skidding noise on the pavement. "I told you to stay away from her. I warned you."

Matt threw a punch, and instead of defending himself, Sculpt pushed me out of the way just before Matt's fist connected with his cheek. I heard the sound of bone smashing into bone.

"No! Matt, no. Please." I scrambled forward just as Sculpt hauled off and hit Matt in return, but his punch was much harder and landed Matt on his ass. "Matt." I ran over and fell onto my knees beside him.

Matt rubbed his jaw then tested it. "Nice punch, asshole." He came to his feet, then helped me to mine. "And now you're out of a gig."

"What? Matt, you hit him first." I pulled on his arm.

Sculpt shrugged. "Your loss, buddy. The club only makes it because of Torn. You want to flounder in shitty-ass bands then go for it." Sculpt stepped forward and got right in Matt's face. "I'm not giving her up. Ever."

My breath hitched, and Matt must have heard, because he glanced at me.

"Shit." He ran his hand through his hair muttering a few choice words under his breath.

"Matt." Sculpt looked at me and then back at Matt. "I want her to come on tour with the band."

My mouth dropped open. We'd never talked about me going with him on tour.

"Jesus," Matt muttered then started pacing. "Emily's like my little sister. And you, Sculpt ... are dangerous. You know why? Because not a single person knows who you are. That's what I don't like, and that's why Emily won't be going anywhere with you."

Sculpt got right up in Matt's face, his voice controlled. "That's her choice to make, not yours." Sculpt didn't wait for a reply as he turned toward his bike. He threw his leg over the seat, then looked at me. "Eme." He disengaged the clutch then pressed the ignition.

I looked from Sculpt's retreating bike to Matt and back again. Oh God. He said I could go with him. He was giving me a choice. But I couldn't. I loved Matt; he'd been there for me growing up, but Sculpt ... Was Sculpt my path ahead? Was I really going to have to choose between them?

"Fuck, Emily." Matt sighed. "You're going to get hurt."

I looked at the ground, because I knew that was a big possibility, and I didn't want him to see the truth in my eyes. Going with Sculpt ... it wasn't an option. I knew that. I had to make it on my own and going with Sculpt would just lead to me being a burden on him. A person he'd have to look after and ruin his chances at stardom. Shit, my mom had said, she couldn't become an architect because she got pregnant with me.

Matt put his arm around me and pulled me into a hug. I rested my cheek against his chest hearing the steady rhythm of his heart. "He scares me, Eme. I asked around, and even his band mates know pretty much nothing about his past. Did he even tell you he and his mother moved here when he was sixteen? Do you know where he lived before? Has he mentioned anything?"

I shook my head.

The hardness suddenly shifted from him, and I saw the vulnerability in his face. The pierced lips softened and curved downward while his shoulders slumped as if his muscles had finally released all their tension. He sighed while he pinched the bridge of his nose.

"You're going to see him anyway, aren't you?" Matt asked, his tone was much softer, resigned.

"Yeah." The knot in my stomach grew tighter. I didn't like hurting Matt, but I needed Sculpt, wanted him. Though I did understand why Matt wanted me to have nothing to do with him.

Matt nodded. "No going to his fights, Emily. That shit is bad news, and I don't want you to be a part of it."

"I want to see his band play." Once. That was all I needed before he left. A memory of him on stage, singing to me with his sexy gravelled voice. Something to hold onto. The knot in my stomach intensified.

Matt ran his hand over the top of his head, back and forth, then groaned. "I can't believe I'm saying this ... I should be firing his ass for blatantly dating you after I told him not to." Matt did know me; when it came to my mind being made up I was stubborn. "Fine. Come to the bar, but Emily please think about what I've said? Maybe if he told you something about himself ..."

I nodded, then I stood on my tip toes and kissed his cheek. "Love you, Matt."

I sat with my phone in my lap and watched *The Walking Dead* while my nerves shot off in all directions waiting for Sculpt to text me after his fight. Not even the blood and guts of my favorite show could stop my mind from thinking about the man who was stealing my heart ... no, he'd already stolen my heart. It was in his grasp; the question was what would he do with it?

Chapter Five

Sculpt was tense, had been ever since the fight three days ago. He'd won, so it wasn't an ego hit, because I knew damn well Sculpt would take a hit if he lost a fight. He was pretty casual when he talked about his fights—until now. I thought I was reading too much into it, but when he passed the ice cream parlor without stopping on the way to the horse farm, I knew whatever was bothering him was big.

Was he thinking about me coming with him on tour? Was he regretting asking me? Had it been a spur of the moment decision because he'd been put on the spot by Matt? No, Sculpt wasn't the type to do anything because of someone else pressuring him.

He drove to our favorite spot, parked his truck on the side of the road, and grabbed his guitar from the back. He came around the truck, took my hand, and we slipped through the fence.

"No ice cream?"

He kept walking, lips pressed together, face tight. "No."

I pulled back. “Is something wrong? You’ve been ... I don’t know ... off since your fight. Is it Matt? Are you changing your mind about us?”

Sculpt set his guitar case on the ground then bent his knees so he became level with me. He cupped my face, and his eyes softened while his thumbs stroked back and forth over my cheeks. His attention made my insides turn to mush. I was sinking further and further into him when he looked all sweet and concerned.

“Eme, I’m not changing my mind. Ever. This has nothing to do with you, okay? It’s just some shit from my past.”

His past? I opened my mouth to ask him but he kissed me, and any insecurity about what was bothering him went flying up into the wind with the dandelion puffs.

“I don’t want you worrying.” His finger traced my lower lip, and I nodded. “Come on. I have a song to finish writing before you see me play.”

We settled on the hill, and I went and spent time with the horses while he fiddled on his guitar. When I came back, I lay on my side in the grass while he played.

When I woke it was dark outside, and I was snuggled in Sculpt’s arms, sitting between his legs, his lean, hard body draped around me. His fingers slowly stroked my outer thigh while his other hand rested on my abdomen, one finger circling my belly button. I turned to look up at him over my shoulder. He was staring out across the moonlit field, observing the horses in the distance.

“Eme.” He leaned into me further and kissed the side of my neck.

“Sorry, I didn’t mean to fall asleep. It must have been your sexy, raspy voice.” I cuddled closer, and his arm tightened. “Did you finish the song?” His guitar lay in its case next to us.

“Yeah, Mouse. It’s good.”

I sat up, excited for him. He’d told me last week that he hadn’t written anything in a year. I had yet to see his band play, and I was excited to hear them, but nervous too. I mean, Sculpt was six foot three and all muscle. And he had ink running down his left arm to his elbow, which made the hot a scary, badass hot. Then put in that fact that he was in a band and did some illegal underground fighting ... Well girls were no doubt all over him, and I wasn't ready to face the reality of what dating Sculpt entailed.

I reached up and ran my finger over the slight indent in his chin. "Can I hear it?"

He shook his head, and despite his lack of smile, because he rarely did smile, I saw the flicker of amusement in his eyes. "No, Eme. You'll hear it with the band on stage, and me singing to you." The amusement left his eyes, and I felt him stiffen. "Did you think about what I asked, Emily?"

I knew exactly what he was referring to. I had a perpetual war in my head for the last three days. I wasn't ready to have my heart blasted with porcupine quills when Sculpt left me to go on tour, but I also wasn't ready to go on the road with a group of guys I hadn't even met yet, and have Sculpt responsible for me. I planned on starting college in a month. I had a life here with Kat and Matt, and even though I didn't want Sculpt to leave, I couldn't see myself leaving either.

"Eme." His arms tightened around me. "Tell me." He shifted, easily picking me up under the arms and bringing me around so I sat facing him, my legs bent on either side of him. It was intimate, and Christ, it was hard to resist him and not just say screw it and tell him how I felt and go with him. "Eme, tell me."

"Tell you what?"

He watched me carefully, eyes never once wavering. "You know what I'm asking, but this once I'll indulge you. Tell me you don't want more."

Shit. He knew I was crazy about him. I'd been trying to keep my feelings ... well hidden, somewhat. It obviously wasn't working. I licked my lips and tried to look away, but he was ready for that and held my head between his hands.

"Eme."

Fuck. I was so not good at this. The last person I expressed my feelings to was my dad while he lay in the hospital dying.

"Mouse." He leaned in, and my hands went to his upper thighs feeling the flex of his muscles beneath my palms. "Look at me." I did. "I want you with me. I'll look after you." His voice lowered. "I'm not happy leaving you here, baby."

And that was the problem; I didn't want to be "looked after." I'd looked after myself all my life. My mom ... I sometimes wondered if she even remembered she had a daughter.

"Emily. I don't play games. I told you what I want, and I know you want me."

I didn't know whether to be pissed or laugh at his arrogance. What I did know was that I was turned on—big time. How could he do that? I mean, he was just looking at me, and yet ... his eyes abducted me. "Sculpt ... I ..."

Sculpt tightened his legs around me. "Eme." He gripped my chin and held me steady. He waited several seconds, and I finally inhaled a shaky breath. "I'll never hurt you. I know you're worried about the women." I opened my mouth to speak, but his eyes narrowed, and I shut it again. "I'm a fighter. I'm in a band. The women will always be there, but I'm with you."

And that was the issue. Why was he with me? I wasn't pretty, had big hips, mousey, brown hair, and my thighs were my best feature. Most guys wouldn't say so, because I was only five foot three, and they liked the tall, skinny fawn-like legs. I liked my thighs, because I rode horses, and they were the most muscular, lean part of my body.

He stiffened, and I recognized the russet in his eyes reflect in the moonlight. I laid my hands flat on his chest feeling his beating heart beneath my touch. "Jesus, Emily, you have to bury that shit your mother tells you. I swear if she wasn't a woman, I'd kick her ass."

I gasped. How did he know about my mother?

"Yeah, Mouse, I know it's swimming around in your head like a shark eating all your confidence. Do you think I don't pay attention? I've asked you about your mother, and I see what it does to you. You spent most of your childhood at Matt and Kat's. A girl doesn't do that if her mother is something special. I'm certain yours is not. She's put toxic shit in your head."

"Sculpt ... I ... my ..." Yeah. I had no words. He was right. My mom was toxic, and that was why I never saw her, not that she'd remember if I did.

He tucked my hair behind my ear. It seemed so natural; I wondered if he even realized he was doing it. "We're exploring this, Eme. I want you on tour with me."

"I need more time, Sculpt. I can't suddenly decide to change my life and go with you. I have school starting and Matt and Kat ..." My voice trailed off.

Silence.

"You want to train horses. Why are you wasting your time going to college taking accounting?"

We'd been through this. "Sculpt, it's a silly dream. I need to focus on what's real, and that is finding a career and making money."

"You're wrong Eme. You should be chasing your dream." He sighed. "I'm leaving. Next week."

My breath hitched, and my heart felt like it had been pierced with quills, and he hadn't even left yet. "But I thought—"

"Things have changed. We're leaving sooner than we planned."

I couldn't go. God, I wanted to, but he needed to live his dream, and I had to make my own way. I never wanted him to regret being with me. Anything I wanted in life I had to reach for myself. I didn't want someone else supporting me. One good thing I'd learned from my mother was that if I wanted anything, I had to get it myself, because she sure as hell wasn't going to give it to me.

"Sculpt. I can't."

"Emily." He lay back in the grass scowling. "You're overthinking this."

"But Sculpt—"

"No buts, Emily. I can't handle any buts. I'm pissed right now."

"But—"

He sat up again, brows lowered. "No."

"But you'll like my but." I leaned toward him and nipped his chin. That got him to ease up, and his muscles relaxed.

"I already like your butt." His hand slid down the small of my back to my ass and squeezed. It was playful, but I could still see the darkness in his eyes, and his face was hard.

"Sculpt. My but is important."

"Yeah Eme, it is." I slapped him on the shoulder, and I was glad when he laughed. "Okay what's your but?"

"I was going to say, *but* ..." His brows rose. "Before you go, I want you to make love to me." I paused, seeing his brows rise with surprise, then I pushed on quickly before I lost my nerve. "Like now, Sculpt. Right now. Here in this spot where we always hang out together. Our place. You with your guitar, and me with the horses."

His hands that were slowly roaming stopped, squeezing my upper thighs, and he stared at me with such intensity that I was getting hot just watching him watch me. "That's your but?"

I nodded.

"I knew I liked your butt." He put his hands on either side of my face and met my eyes. "If you're in my bed ... you're not in anyone else's. You got that, Mouse? Even if I can't convince you in the next week to come with me—no one else's."

"Okay. Same goes for you." Surrounded by women night after night would be a lot harder for him than for me.

Sculpt stroked the side of my face. "Emily. You erase the bad in my life."

I couldn't imagine Sculpt having any bad. He was hot, had an incredible voice, had a body that was no doubt in the dictionary under the definition for muscle.

He may not laugh often, but when he did it was magical and made up for all the other times he didn't. I sensed the hardness in him, the untouchable part that he refused to let me discover, but we'd only known one another for a couple months.

His thumb caressed my lips, and the ache between my legs intensified. My stomach wasn't just pretty little butterflies; it was a flock of Egrets taking flight.

He picked me up and set me on the grass beside him then got on his knees in front of me. He tilted forward, and I leaned back until I was resting in the grass, and he was hovering above.

My nerves were sparking off in every direction while the twinge between my legs became a spasm of aching need. I was breathing so fast that it was like I'd run a marathon.

"Have you ever been touched, Emily?"

I shook my head, too breathless to respond verbally.

"If you're not ready ... tell me now. Be damn sure about this, Eme."

He was dead serious, and it sent a strange thrill through me. I didn't want to wait. I wanted him here and now with the wind against my skin, being in my favorite place in the world with Sculpt. "I don't want to wait."

His hand swept into my hair and weaved through the strands. His fingers tightened, and he pulled back, and my breath hitched. "I'm tasting your pussy. Then Emily, I'm going to fuck you until you scream. Does that make you nervous? Because you're trembling all over."

"Yeah," I whispered.

"Yeah, nervous? Or yeah you're going to scream when I sink inside of you for the first time?"

"Yeah, to all of it." I'd wanted Sculpt since the night I met him. Needed him. It was like I had been living with anticipation for this moment my entire life. It scared the hell out me. What if I sucked at it? What if we were incompatible? What if it was awkward?

"I want you screaming and quivering. And baby, you should be nervous ... because I plan on changing your mind and having you begging me to take you on tour." The corners of his lips twitched, and my insides lit up. I couldn't help but think about what he could do to me, how I'd say goodbye when it was time for him to leave. "You're Lego building, Emily. Rethinking your decision?"

I jerked and met his eyes. There it was—his eyes dancing with laughter and desire, a sexy combination that had me tightening my grip on his biceps.

He didn't wait for my reply. "Too late, Mouse. You're mine."

He tilted his head like he always did before he kissed me, and claimed my lips. And he did claim, devour, and feed the hunger we both felt between us. Heat flowed over my skin as if the afternoon sun was beaming down on it. Little sparks tap-danced shivers through my body. There was no hesitation in what he was taking, what he wanted, and I fell into his kiss like melted butter.

His hands stroked up my sides then down again. "God, these curves."

He groaned, and the vibration sent my heart rate spiking. My hands found their way into his hair, pulling him closer, harder. God, I needed him. It was like I was breathing for this man. It wasn't normal. Was this normal? Did it matter?

"Sculpt."

He took my hands and placed them above my head, locking them down with his own. "Logan. Call me Logan, Eme."

Oh God. His name. He told me his real name. "Logan," I said and heard him groan.

"Again."

"Logan."

His lips trailed succulent kisses down my throat, his teeth nipping, then his tongue licking to take away the bite. "I want you to call me that whenever we're alone, Emily. Call me Logan."

"Okay." It was a whispered moan mixed with a sigh. Eyes closed, head thrown back, I edged my legs out from under him on either side and wrapped them around his hips. He grunted as I clenched, hoping to ease the ache, but all I did was make it more intense. More aware.

"Oh God, Logan, please. I need you." We could savor and taste and discover one another the rest of the week, but right now I wanted Logan inside me. I wanted to feel him naked against me. It was like waiting at the top of a toboggan hill and being rocked back and forth before being pushed over the edge.

"I know, Mouse." He nipped at my ear lobe then suckled, and I fought against his hands that kept me pinned to the grass.

I had to touch him, feel his skin, get rid of the clothes that separated us. "Logan please. Clothes."

His head came up from him kissing my collar bone. "We're taking this slow. My way. I've waited too long to have you right where you are now, under me, pussy aching, hot and sexy as hell."

I'd never been called sexy in my life and it sent a shudder straight through me hearing it from Logan.

"I like to play, Emily. It's who I am. And it's in you too. I know you get turned on when I take control." Did I? I wasn't experienced enough to really know what he was talking about. "But if you're scared of anything, I need you to say no. That's all it takes, and we stop. Understand?"

I got what he was saying. I mean, I wasn't oblivious to sex. I knew "play" could mean a few things, and it made me nervous and excited at the same time.

He let go of my wrists, and I put my hands on his abdomen and lifted his shirt inch by inch. Logan hovered over me, watching my eyes. I saw him suck in air and close his eyes for a second when my hands crept up his chest then slowly caressed his nipples.

I kept my eyes on him, loving his reaction. Loving how my touch was driving him crazy. My fingertips traced every muscle on his chest then down to his abdomen. Every contour was a new mountain for me to explore. I was panting, and Logan had his eyes closed and was breathing harder than I was.

"Shirt, Logan." I lifted it upward, and he succumbed to my bribe and threw off his shirt. My hands went to the button on his jeans, and he grabbed my hands and stilled them.

"No. I let you play so you could relax. Now it's me." Within seconds he had my shirt up, over my head, and his fingers were working at my bra. The snaps gave, and my breasts fell from their confines into his hands. *"Emily."*

"Yes," I whispered.

He lowered his body, and then his tongue circled my nipple while his hands caressed my side, down to my hip then back up again to tease my breasts. My body was exploding with sensations, pain as he bit my nipple, then pleasure as he suckled sweetly and licked the sensitive skin with heated moisture.

I gripped his hair, eyes closed and body arching into him as he sent me into a furnace of heat. Getting myself off to him couldn't even begin to compete with the real thing.

He moved lower, soft kisses trailing down my chest to my stomach. "This. And this." He slid his hand to my hip. "I love everything about your body." His kisses went further, and my body was already anticipating him. Ache was no longer a word associated with what he was doing to me; it was much, much more than that.

My hands curled in the grass, and I moaned as his fingers undid my jeans.

The button popped.

The slow descend of my zipper drove me crazy.

The sound was agonizing, because I wanted him to rip them off and plunge deep inside of me, hard and fast. But Logan wanted to do this slowly. Relish every moment, and yet, I was dying for him.

"Logan." My whispered moan was met with a muffled, "Christ" as I felt his fingers reach in my jeans and go lower. And lower until—

I stiffened, sucking in air.

"You're wet."

Well, yeah, I'd been wet for two-and-half months. Logan turned me on just by looking at me. I ran my hands through his sexy bedroom hair. "I've been wet since the day I met you, Logan."

His head came up, and his eyes widened. God, he had to have known how much I wanted him.

"Jesus, Emily." He kissed me again, hands curled into my hair, and his mouth hard against mine. There was no breathing, no thinking, just pure hunger.

He raised his head, both of us breathing hard, his hair falling in front of his right eye while he looked at me with haunted openness. "I'm not letting you go."

I cupped his cheek with my shaking hand, my thumb stroking across his stubble. "Don't ever hurt me."

"Never." He sat up then moved down me as he grabbed the edges of my jeans and pulled. I lifted my butt, and my panties came with the denim.

He stopped at mid-thigh. "Beautiful. And shaved. That is a ... surprise."

I did have a small, what they call, landing strip, but the rest was waxed clean—Brazilian. I'd never liked hair down there, and Logan liking it—it made me giddy inside.

His fingertip ran down the small patch of hair, and I gasped as he spread the folds then slipped into the wetness.

"Logan, oh God," I arched my back, trying to bend my knees but unable to because of my jeans trapping my legs. "Jeans, Logan. Jeans."

"Wait." He continued to enjoy caressing my clit until I screamed and panted, then when he felt me close to the edge, he backed off and went further down to circle my opening.

I wanted him inside me so bad that I was arching up to meet him until he put his hand on my stomach and forced me to stay down.

He put two fingers on either side of my folds, slid through the wetness then hesitated at my opening.

"Logan. Please."

"Beg me."

"Logan."

"Emily."

"Please, Logan. I'm begging you."

He plunged two fingers inside, and I inhaled sharply at the sudden assault. It grabbed me. Held me. It didn't let go.

He pulled out, and I cried out with disappointment only to be met with a quick kiss on the top of my clit. Then he tore my jeans off the rest of the way and lay between my legs.

"Bend your knees."

I did.

"Open. Wide."

I did that too. I trusted him implicitly and him taking control felt like it was fulfilling a need in me to surrendered to him. I was able to forget everything and bask in whatever pleasure he gave me.

He gently pushed them a little wider still, and I closed my eyes and bit my lip as I felt the first suckle on my clit. Oh God. The sensations inside me were so heightened that I knew I wasn't going to last more than a few minutes with Logan's mouth on me. Never had I imagined it being like this. I moaned, arching my back as Logan's tongue slipped inside me.

Gripping the grass on either side of my head I groaned as he worked magic with his tongue through the folds, tasting the wetness then suckling my clit again. The pressure in my abdomen ached, built, and was cresting. I tensed. So, so close to the edge, nearly pushed off the hill.

He stopped. "Not yet, baby."

Oh God, how could I do that? "Logan, I can't. I can't hold—"

"You will." His voice was rough and demanding, and it made me even hotter. His fingers pushed inside me. "So tight."

He pumped in and out of me several times then licked me again. "Your pussy is perfect. I knew you'd taste this way. You're made for me, Emily."

"Logan," I panted, every muscle tightening. "Please. I need you inside me now."

He pulled his fingers from me, and then I watched as he licked them off one by one. I nearly came just watching him. The way his eyes glued to mine; seeing right into me. How the curve of his mouth partially crept up to a smile as he tasted me.

It was him. Everything he did, I adored. How he walked with confidence, not a swagger, but when he came into a room it was with presence. How he was chasing his dream with his band, willing to take all the money he had to try and make it in a business that was saturated with great bands. He took risks because he had faith in himself. How he didn't take shit from anyone. How he put all of himself into whatever he was doing. But most of all, I loved how he looked at me and saw everything I am and could be.

"Are you on something?"

I nodded. "The pill. To control my ovulation pain."

"I'm clean. I was checked two weeks after I met you and have been with no one since."

He'd been with no one. He went and got checked? Was it because he thought ... was he thinking about us?

"Yeah, Emily. I wanted to make sure I was good before I ever touched you, condom or not."

Wow. "I want you inside me, Logan. I want to feel all of you."

He leaned to the side and yanked off his jeans. I glanced down before he moved on top of me and glimpsed his erection—

pulsating, huge—and wondered how the hell that was fitting inside me. Before I could start Lego building and scaring myself, I reached between us and touched him.

"Eme," he murmured as my fingers curled around him then stroked every inch of him.

His penis was throbbing and hot, and as I caressed, his eyes closed, and his head tilted back as he groaned.

"Stop. Fuck. I'm going to come before I'm even inside you." He grabbed his cock and rubbed it between my legs, the wetness clinging to him. "I'll go slow, Mouse."

My hand reached up to lock my fingers in his hair. "No, go fast. Just get that part over with."

"No." His voice was hard and firm. "You're going to remember this, and not with pain." His mouth descended as he sunk lower, his cock nudging my opening.

Wrapping my legs around his waist and my arms around his back, I pressed upward with my hips, and the tip pressed against my barrier. I couldn't get him in any further, and my body was aching so bad I was going to scream.

He tore his mouth away from mine and grabbed my chin. "Look at me, Emily. I want to see you when I take you. I want to watch you while you scream my name."

"Logan."

He pushed his hips forward and moved in me a little further. I could feel him stretching my hymen, and I was sure he could too. He gripped my chin to make certain I didn't move then rotated his hips and withdrew, and I moaned.

"Slow, Eme."

He moved inside me again, and this time he kept going until I felt a sudden sharp pain.

Fuck. Shit. It hurt.

And yet ... him erect and full inside me was ... it was so connecting and surreal.

He leaned in and kissed me while he was sunk deep inside. A slow languished kiss that had me forgetting about the pain and instead filling me with a new urgency. I wanted him to move.

"Logan." God, I needed him to move. I pushed upward, and he sunk even deeper. Yes, God yes.

"You good?"

The tenderness was overridden by the aching need. I nodded, and he began to move. I clenched my legs around him, ankles crossed on his back, both of us panting, our eyes locked on one another.

"You're mine, Emily." He moved harder, faster, and I tried to close my eyes, but he grabbed my chin. "Look at me."

Each push brought us closer; I was on edge, ready, the ache heightened to a place it could go no further. He pressed his hips in an upward motion so he rubbed against my clit, and a jolt went through me, then another and another. The intense building inside was too much.

He pressed harder.

"Oh God. Logan. Logan." I let go, my eyes squeezing shut. "Logan!" I screamed as everything in my body exploded into tiny bursts.

"Emily." He pumped harder, the smack of flesh on flesh loud. He thrust deeper. Then he took my mouth with an insane hunger as his body stopped pumping, and his muscles tightened while his body shook.

"Mouse." He fell to the side and brought me with him so I was snug to his chest, my legs tangled within his. "Emily. You're a fuckn' trophy. My trophy."

I closed my eyes, head resting on his chest next to my hand.

He leaned upward and kissed my head while his hand stroked up and down my arm. His other hand linked with my fingers on his chest.

"Logan?"

"Yeah, baby."

"Um, someone is watching us."

Logan looked up, and we both started laughing as the appaloosa stared down at us.

Chapter Six

"Oh my God, look at you. You're lit up like a friggin' firecracker. What has Sculpt done to you ... besides break your virginity condom." I hadn't given Kat any details, but I'd told her we'd had sex, and that it was amazing. "Matt's finally resigned to the fact that you and Sculpt are together."

I was a little giddy. Okay, I was super giddy after two nights ago in the horse field. Yesterday, I'd managed to spill four coffees, and bumped into Georgie three times making her spill hers. To say I was day dreaming was an understatement ... I became the daydream. Georgie sent me home early, said I was between my legs and to go get fucked before I had an orgasm while serving coffee to some poor sap who wasn't getting any.

Unfortunately, Logan couldn't see me last night, because the band was polishing up the new song he wanted me to hear tonight.

Kat was wearing a tight blue dress, dipped low, clinging to every inch of her body, down to her mid-thighs. Her stiletto heels lengthened her already long legs, and she had on a silver anklet made up of loops of interlocking circles.

I wore a new dress I'd purchased yesterday after work, and it had been a long process considering Kat had been with me. I must have tried on at least forty dresses before we settled on one. It was white, not stark white, but more of an eggshell and was just as delicate with how tight it was. A classy, sexy look, Kat called it. Parts of it were lace and others silk with a plunging neckline, embracing my body right to mid-thigh.

"Man, he is going to fuck up his lines when he sees you in that," Kat said as I slipped on my heels—also new. "I can't wait to see his face. And make sure he sees your ass."

I laughed. I felt kind of sexy. Most of the time I was in jeans, and this was the nicest piece of clothing I owned. I saved my money for the horses, not clothes or girly stuff.

"I'm just excited to finally hear the band. He talks about them all the time, and I've only met Kite, the drummer." I had yet to mention that Sculpt wanted me to go with them on tour. I didn't think there was any point when I'd decided it wasn't going to happen.

"Matt says they're going to make it big. And by the looks of your boyfriend alone ... Yeah, they're making it." Kat tugged my hand. "Come on. Let's cause some hard-ons."

There was only one man I'd like to cause a hard-on, and there would be no touching him until later tonight.

When we arrived, Torn had yet to take the stage. I was nervous about seeing Sculpt, and my limbs felt like warm pudding. I wasn't sure if the light-headedness was from the two shots Kat and I did before we left the house or my nerves. I was a little scared ... okay terrified of seeing him and close to saying screw college, Kat, and Matt.

Kat snagged a couple drinks from Brett the bartender, then we moved through the crowd to a spot near the stage. "It's packed. Wow, Torn draws a lot of people." Kat winked. "Sculpt's one hot piece of ass, and he's all yours, Eme."

I chugged back my beer, quenching my dry mouth. I kept looking around, wondering if I'd get the chance to see him before he went on stage. We'd only texted a few times yesterday, because he was busy with the band, but he never forgot to send me a text before bed. I couldn't sleep anymore without it, Logan's good night—*dream sweet, Emily*.

My cell vibrated.

You good, Mouse?

I smiled, and the tension eased from my shoulders. I could picture him with his hand on the back of my neck, fingers wrapped in my hair as he looked down at me.

Yeah. Waiting impatiently to hear you sing like the rest of your fans.

I hesitated for a second, afraid of being vulnerable, but then decided if I couldn't let him know now, then he would never know before he left. I typed and sent the next message, before I could talk myself out of it.

I think I like you too much. And I missed seeing you yesterday. I think I'm addicted to you.

There was a long pause, and I wanted to kick myself for telling him I missed him and was addicted to him. I mean, what guy wanted to hear that? I was still cautious about keeping my feelings contained, afraid if he knew how hard I'd fallen he'd be bumping up his tour date. I started to get nervous when he didn't respond, and I kept my eyes glued to my dark screen.

Suddenly, it lit up.

Look up.

I stared at the screen for a second then looked up.

He was standing there, a few feet away, his hands shoved in his front pockets of his jeans, hair falling across his left eye. He wore a simple white T-shirt which accentuated his tattoos down his left arm.

My breath hitched as he stared at me, and everything inside me went fragile as I realized that I'd already fallen—hard.

I stood.

Then I walked toward him. My heart soared when I saw his eyes widen at the sight of my dress. He took me in from head to toe, and the inferno in his eyes could've set an entire city on fire. And it was because of me. I did that to him.

I stopped inches away.

He reached out and caressed the side of my face. "Eme."

I was breathless, and my knees weakened. I so had to make certain I was sitting when he sang. His other hand rested on my hip, and he slowly stroked up to my waist and back down.

"You take my breath away." He tilted his head and leaned in close to whisper in my ear, "I missed you too, baby. I want you coming with us. Some guy wanting in your pants, and I'm hundreds of miles away ... I don't like it, Eme."

"Sculpt, I'm capable of keeping a guy off me. Remember, you taught me the moves. I'm good at it now."

His palm cupped my chin, and he raised my head. "Yeah, you're good." Then he gave me sweet, and I melted into his sweet as he kissed my lips, slow and lingering, like he was making love to me right there in front of everyone.

"The new song tonight, it's for you, Eme." When his lips lowered onto mine it was like all indecision was taken away. There was softness in him, the way he cradled me, how his eyes never faltered when he looked at me.

When I breathed in, it was him I inhaled. I was completely in love with him, and he was leaving in five days.

He rested his forehead against mine. "I need to get ready. We're together tonight, Emily. Just us. Okay?"

"Okay."

When he walked away, I felt Kat's hand on the small of my back. "That guy is so in love with you. Damn, missy, a sweet package of ass, face, voice, and those words he just spilled to you ? ... Jealous here."

"I'm in love with him."

She laughed. "Um, yeah ... Obvious."

I gasped, flinging around. "Oh God, do you think he can tell?"

"Missy, he damn well better. You're like maple syrup at his feet." She snagged the two new beers from our table and passed me one. She grinned, brows rising. "To getting fucked by sweet and spicy."

We finished our beers, and Matt came over and told us Torn would be on in five, so I started for the washroom, before they came on stage. I didn't want to miss a single second of Logan singing.

"Missy," Kat called after me. I looked over my shoulder smiling. I was buzzed and happy. Yeah, I was really happy. Logan was going to sing, and then we were going to a hotel for the night, and I loved him, and Kat said he loved me. I had five days left with him, and I was going to make certain it was spent with him in my arms. "You're beautiful," Kat called.

"Fuck yeah." Some guy shouted.

God, I loved my bestie. And for once, I felt beautiful.

I weaved through the crowd then made my way down the hallway to the washroom. I never saw him come up behind me, maybe because I was still thinking about Logan, and my mind was thinking about him in a hotel room—with me.

It happened within seconds. I had my hand on the bathroom door, and an arm hooked around my waist. As I sucked in air to tell the guy to screw off, I breathed in a sweet pungent smell as a linen cloth was forced over my nose and mouth.

Then darkness.

The beginning

Acknowledgements

I feel like I've been handed a gift finding Debra from The Book Enthusiast Promotions. She is my forever girl and my books will go nowhere else from now on. She has been is so supportive with this journey of both "With You" and "Torn from You". You're the best Debra. Thank you!

Kari. Wow. My cover design girl who saw my vision and brought it! To all the beasts being friends and plenty of Dyson's.

I also want to thank Black Firefly for proof reading "With You". You fit me in your tight schedule and helped me give the readers a polished novella.

About the Author

Nashoda Rose lives in Toronto with her assortment of pets. She writes contemporary romance with a splash of darkness, or maybe it's a tidal wave. Her novel "Torn from You" is the first in the Tear Asunder series. When she isn't writing, she can be found sitting in a field reading with her dog at her side while her horses graze nearby. She loves interacting with her readers on Facebook and chatting about her addiction—books.

53097444R00041

Made in the USA
Charleston, SC
05 March 2016